This book belongs to:

_____

To all of the
Dreamers,
have fun creating.
We sure are!

Frankie the seagull was born and raised on the sandy beach shores. He loves to watch the people as they come from far and wide. Every time they pack to leave he feels a sadness deep inside. As he sees the cars pull away, he pretends he is along for the ride.

Frankie has big dreams. He can't quite explain what they are or when they started. He's always had this pull to live a different life. He is grateful for his life at the beach. The beach is all he has ever known. Yet he still feels that there is something more, something better out in that great big world to explore.

He knows that most of the gulls in his life
won't understand or they will think his
thoughts are foolish.

He has one friend he can talk to about it;
Trixie the crab. It is an unlikely friendship
that has grown into a strong alliance.

One day, Frankie was feeling very brave. He was with his
mom and dad and blurted out, "I have big dreams!"

His parents stopped and stared. Then his mom looked at
him and said, "Well, go on."

Frankie took a big breath in as he began, "I want to fly to the
north and breathe the mountain air. I want to see the forests
and the animals there. I want to dip my wings under the
waterfall. I want to sit in canopies and feel super tall." He
was smiling as he spoke; as he saw it in his mind.

His dad said, "You're a seagull Frankie, this is where you
belong. End of story!"

Then his mom chimed in and said, "You can't leave here and
do all of that. Remove those silly dreams from your head!"

Frankie, wishing he had kept his dreams to himself, flew to the other side of the beach. Back and forth he paced, kicking the sand. Feeling the shift in vibrations, Trixie crawled out to the surface.

"Oh, hey Frankie," she said. "What's happening?"

"I just told my parents about my big dreams. And... well, it could have gone better," shrugged Frankie.

"Frankie, your dreams are beautiful and I know that if you want it, you will find a way to make it happen. I believe in you!" Trixie exclaimed.

"Thanks, Trixie, you always understand," said Frankie with bright eyes. "I just can't give up on my dreams. I don't care what they say. I am going to fly free from here one day."

From that day forward, Frankie ONLY talked to Trixie about his dreams. He didn't want anyone telling him it was impossible. He knew that as long as he imagined it, ANYTHING IS POSSIBLE.

So he dreamed and dreamed. He flew all over in his mind; to the mountains and the valleys, through the forests and the streams.

"Keep it alive, Frankie," he'd say to himself. "Fly onward toward your dreams."

Finally, one day, Frankie made the decision that it was time for his great adventure.

"I love you Mom and Dad. See you around Trixie," Frankie said as he flew on by. "I'm off for my great adventure, I will share stories from far and wide."

"WE LOVE YOU SON," his mom and dad squawked as loud as could be, "Go be free."

"Byeeeeee, good luck," squeaked Trixie with excitement.

Frankie flew left. Frankie flew right.

He flew high.

And he flew low.

He was so proud of himself for starting his journey.
He flew and flew, until suddenly, he was drawn in by
these tall bright lights, with a vulture sitting on top.

"Mind if I share this space with you?" Frankie asked.

"Please, come," said Vulture, "I never mind company."

And just like that, Frankie's first perching place was the stadium lights of a baseball game. As he and Vulture were sharing stories and dreams, Frankie saw something flying in from the distance.

Vulture, seeing what it was said, "Oh that is the red-tailed hawk. My cue to take off. Pleasure meeting you Frankie, have fun following your dreams."

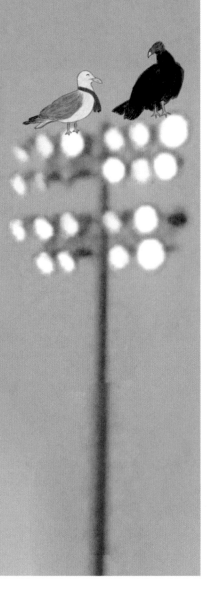

Hawk landed next to Frankie. He and Hawk spent quite some time sharing their stories. At one point a ball came flying toward them and Hawk hollered at Frankie, "DUCK!"

Frankie looked around for a duck. When he realized what was happening he quickly opened his mouth wide and caught the ball! He spit it out, shook his head, and said, "Wow! Baseball is exciting!"

He enjoyed the ball game and hearing about the city from Vulture and Hawk, but he knew this wasn't the 'home' he was looking for.

"Thanks for the chat," Frankie said as he stretched his wings. "Time for me to take flight again in search of my dreams."

He flew and flew until he saw beautiful snow-capped mountains.

The mountains were breathtaking, a bit chilly, and to his surprise, he didn't find any animals to sit and chat with. After some exploring, Frankie decided that this wasn't the place for him either. He did not get discouraged, for he knew this was part of the journey to finding what he was seeking; a place that brought peace and pure positive joy.

As he took off from the mountains he looked to see what all was below him. All of a sudden he saw the most beautiful waterfall he had ever seen. He circled around, as though an airplane waiting to land, taking it all in while riding the breeze.

"This," Frankie thought, "is well worth a landing."

He looked ahead and saw that the waterfall was right in front of him. With a big smile on his face, he flew towards it, swooping down to fly through. The sun hit the droplets and Frankie glided through a rainbow to dip his wings into the waterfall.

The moment felt magical.

He didn't know it yet, but he had stumbled upon a special place.

As Frankie was basking in the beauty, he
noticed a frog across the way. He decided to
go say hello.

"Hi, I'm Frankie. This place is so beautiful,
calm, and quiet. I've never seen anything
quite like it," he said to the frog with wonder.

"Hi there Frankie," Frog quipped, "They call
me Niki. I am the greeter and keeper of this
space. Since you are new here, let me tell you
all about it."

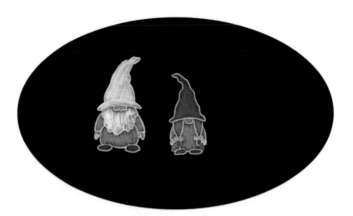

Frankie focused on Niki's every word. He spoke of this magical world, hidden deep in the forest, where many creatures lived. They have always been, and will always be, waiting to be seen.

Niki told Frankie about the sprites, gnomes, elves, and all of Nature's creations. He said they all live in harmony with one another.

"They don't always let themselves be seen," he said, "You have to believe they exist first."

"I believe," Frankie said.

"We thought you might," 3 tiny voices sang out. "I'm Shay and over here we have Fern and Quill."

Frankie was in awe as he watched 3 little sprites that appeared as if they had been there all along.

"Welcome to the forest and our home," they rang in unison. "Relax, enjoy, explore. Stay as long as you desire."

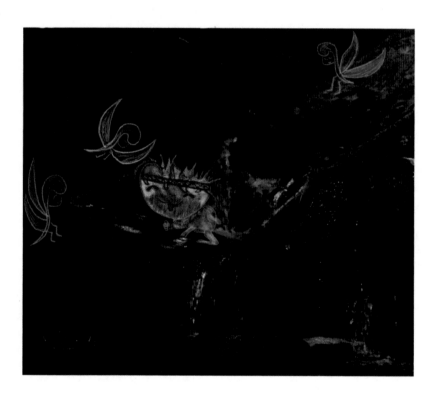

Shay and Fern taught Frankie about the forest fungi or mushrooms as you may know them. There are so many out there, good and bad for you, that he decided it is best just not to eat any. The mushrooms are also where many beings live, it is best not to touch.

Quill showed him a few neat little creatures. A snail and a slug.

"So slimy," said Frankie as he touched the slug with his beak.

A little while later, everyone took Frankie to see where
they made their homes. He loved their tiny tucked
away spaces.

He had only been there a short while, but after talking with Niki, Shay, Fern, and Quill, Frankie felt so alive. Newly awakened at this moment he knew he belonged.

"I am so happy and grateful to share this home with you!" Frankie said with glee.

"YIPEE!!" Everyone shouted.

They all sat around sharing stories as well as praise and thanks for Nature's creations surrounding them.

"Whatever your dreams may be, you can do it,"
Frankie boldly stated. "Just look at me. I took a big
chance and now I'm much more than a gull of the sea."

And with that Frankie flew up to the tallest canopy to
begin building his nest.

Stay tuned for
more books

Follow us
on
Facebook

Contact us:
bubbleshoneypot@gmail.com

https://fb.me/BubblesHoneypot

To order additional copies
visit Amazon.com

Made in the USA
Monee, IL
06 September 2021